Curiosity this big ～～～ in a girl this small!

by Metroni

A
Dash
Story

Publisher - A Dash Story

Bubu
Written by Metroni
Illustrated by Behager Lij

Published by A Dash Story
ISBN: 979-8-218-81297-3
Printed in USA
Falls Church, Virginia

For all the curious kids,
to the dreamers, the doers,
and the little explorers of life,
and for the grown-ups
who still carry that spark.

Bubu is a bright, fearless little girl with small feet and big dreams.

She loves exploring the world around her and never waits for permission.

When a question pops into her mind, she dives in to find the answer.

Her parents guide her through little messes, and her big brother makes her toys.

Bubu loves trying new things. After the rain, she builds a boat for Ants, dam for Frogs, and jumps as high as the grasshoppers.

Bubu learns by doing.

Sometimes Bubu's experiment get messy. she once made a flour glue... and it covered everything!
another day, she drew over the bedroom wall and admired her crayon masterpiece... until her dad walked in. He sighed, grabbed a brush, and painted the wall back to plain white.

But Bubu keeps trying.
Every mess is a new lesson.

One sunny afternoon,
Bubu played under a big tree in her backyard with
colorful toys her big brother made. The warm
breeze carried the smell of flowers, and red,
purple, and yellow petals danced like a rainbow. On the balcony,
her family enjoyed Ethiopian coffee and quiet moments together.

Suddenly, Bubu saw a bird like no other. Its feathers sparkled with golden light, its forehead was deep blue like the early sky, and its back was bright green like leaves after rain. It was so beautiful, Bubu couldn't believe her eyes. What kind of bird was this? She couldn't wait to find out!

The bird landed on the grass and began pecking at seeds and insects.

Bubu's curious mind raced. What if this beautiful bird became my best friend? She imagined feeding it yummy treats, giving it a cozy spot to rest, and keeping it safe. Bubu knew she could make it feel happy and loved. She tiptoed closer, but each time she got near, the bird flapped its wings and flew away!

Bubu waited for hours, hoping the bird would return. But as the sky darkened, it never came back. Feeling sad, she walked home, thinking of ways to bring her new friend back.

That night, Bubu lay in bed, thinking about the golden-feathered bird. She tossed and turned, trying to come up with a plan. After hours of thinking, a spark lit up in her mind. She sat up, eyes wide, I've got it!

Would it work?

13

The next morning, Bubu woke up early and gathered what she needed: a rope, a stick, some seeds, and a bowl. She tied the rope to the bowl, balanced it on the stick, and sprinkled seeds underneath, hoping the bird would come. If it did, she'd pull the rope, drop the bowl, and gently trap it inside. She set the trap by the big tree, and waited.

After waiting for hours, Bubu saw a flash of golden feathers. The bird came closer, its eyes on the seeds. It stepped under the bowl and began pecking, unaware of the trap. Bubu held her breath, gripped the rope, and pulled, the bowl dropped!

Bubu gently carried the bird to her room and placed it in a cozy nest. She gave it food, water, and a soft towel to keep it warm. That night, she sang to the bird and whispered kind words. As the room grew quiet, Bubu drifted into sleep, still watching over her new friend.

The next morning, Bubu woke up excited to see the bird. She offered seeds and water, but it just sat there, quiet and still. Bubu had hoped to hear its song. The silence made her a little worried. Just then, her mom opened the door to wake her up for breakfast and froze.

"Bubu, how did this bird end up in your room?"

Bubu excitedly told her mom how she caught the bird, fed it, and sang to it. Her mom smiled and asked gently, "Do you think the bird feels happy here, Bubu?"

Bubu sighed. "I gave it everything, Mama. But it still looks sad."

Her mom asked, "Do you know why?"

Bubu shook her head. "I don't know why."

Her mother smiled gently. "The bird is sad because you took away its most important gift and gave it things that don't matter as much..."

Bubu frowned. "What did I take?"

"You gave it food and songs," her mother said, "but what it truly needs is to be free."

24

Bubu asked, "What is freedom, Mama?"

Her mom thought for a moment, then tied Bubu's legs with a soft cloth. She gave her toys and snacks, but when Bubu tried to play, she couldn't move.

Bubu looked at her mother and pleaded, "Mama, please untie me! Why did you do that?"

Her mother smiled. "My sunshine, now you know how the bird feels." She pointed to the bird. "It's an Ethiopian Bee- eater, bright, joyful, and free. But when you put it in a nest, you took away its freedom... just like I took yours."

Bubu's heart felt heavy. She gently picked up the bird and carried it outside, feeling its tiny heartbeat. With a deep breath, she opened the nest. The bird paused, then spread its golden wings. With one strong flap, it soared into the sky, free and happy. Bubu watched in awe as it disappeared, its colors dancing in the sun.

From that day, Bubu played under the big tree, watching the bird return every day to sing its sweet song. Bubu and the bird became best friends, and she learned the true meaning of kindness and freedom.

Hi, I'm Metroni!

I grew up with stories told under the bright African sky, in (Ethiopia), one of the last generations to run barefoot under the sun with dusty knees and ashy feet, chasing stories that floated through the wind. in the colors of the sky, the laughter of children, and the rhythm of everyday life. Now, I love turning those memories into adventures that inspire kids to stay curious and brave, just like Bubu!

When I'm not writing or dreaming up new stories, I'm usually busy creating designs and building ideas, because, deep down, I love making things stand tall and strong (yes, even real buildings).

🌟 Bubu's next adventure is on the way!

Follow the fun at www.adashstory.com
and on Instagram @adash_story

A Dash Story